I Love You, Stinky Face

Written by Lisa McCourt

Illustrated by Cyd Moore

Troll

BridgeWater Books

For Aimee ～ L.M.

For my most wonderful ones,
Lindsay and Branden ～ C.M.

This edition published in 2002.

Copyright © 1997 by Lisa McCourt. Reprinted
by permission of Troll Communications L.L.C. All rights reserved.

Reprinted by permission of BridgeWater Books.

Printed in Belgium.

10   9   8   7   6

Library of Congress Cataloging-in-Publication Data

McCourt, Lisa.
      I love you, Stinky Face / written by Lisa McCourt ; illustrated by Cyd Moore.
          p.   cm.
      Summary : A mother and child discuss how the mother's love would remain constant
even if her child were a stinky skunk, scary ape, or bug-eating green alien.
      ISBN 0-8167-4392-4
      [l. Mother and child–Fiction.   2. Animals–Fiction.]   I. Moore, Cyd. ill.   II. Title.
PZ7.M1374SIf 1997
[E]–dc21   97-10017

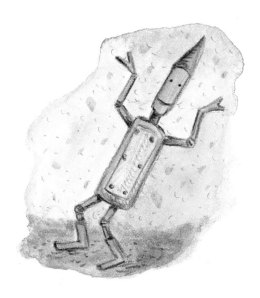

"I love you, my wonderful child," said Mama as she tucked me in.
But I had a question.

Mama, what if I were a big scary

"If you were a big, scary ape, I would comb your whole hairy self to make sure you didn't have any tangles.

Happy Birthday! Happ

"And I would make your birthday cake out of bananas, and I would tell you, 'I love you, my big, scary ape.'"

But, Mama, but, Mama, what if I were a super smelly skunk, and I smelled so bad that my name was Stinky Face?

"Then I would give you a bath and sprinkle you with sweet-smelling powder.

"And if you still smelled bad, I wouldn't mind, and I would hug you tight and whisper in your ear, 'I love you, Stinky Face.'"

But, Mama, but, Mama, what if I were an alligator with big, sharp teeth that could bite your head off?

"Then I would buy you a bigger toothbrush for your big teeth and make sure that you brushed them every night so they'd stay healthy and strong.

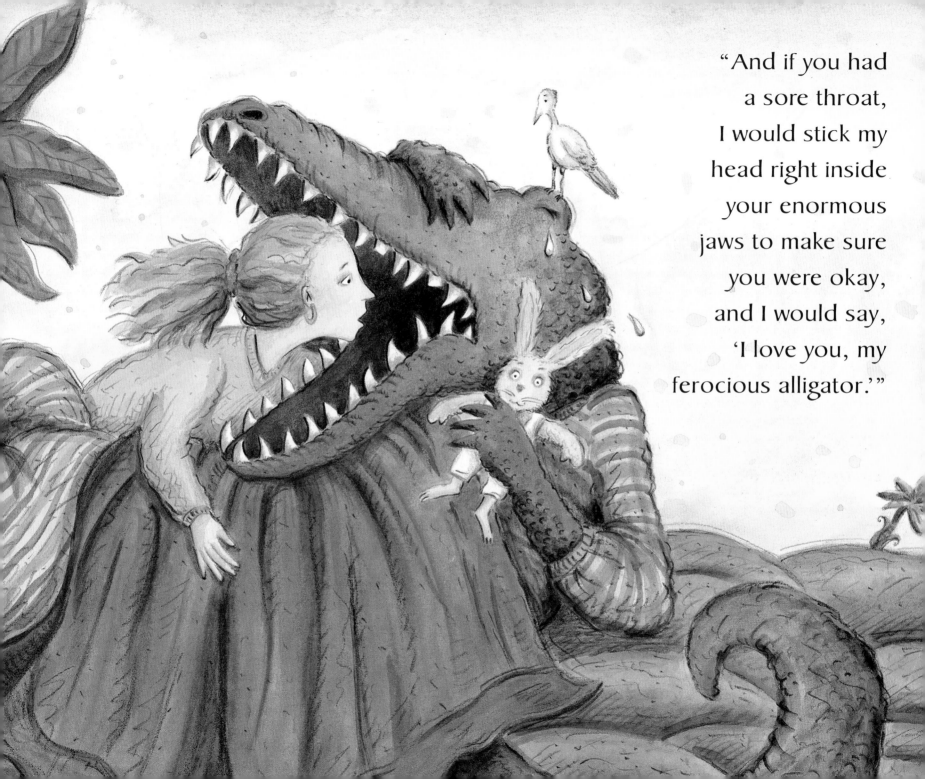

"And if you had a sore throat, I would stick my head right inside your enormous jaws to make sure you were okay, and I would say, 'I love you, my ferocious alligator.'"

But, Mama, what if I were a terrible meat-eating dinosaur with razor-sharp claws that ripped my sheets to shreds every night while I slept?

"Then I would give you plenty of meat to eat, if that is what you liked. And I would sew your sheets back together every day, because, after all, ripping them would be an accident.

"And I would tuck you into your newly mended sheets every night and say, 'I love you, my sweet, terrible dinosaur.'"

But, Mama, but, Mama, what if I were a swamp creature with slimy, smelly seaweed hanging from my body, and I couldn't ever leave the swamp or I would die?

"Then I would build a house right next to the swamp, and I would stay with you and take care of you always. And when you splashed to the surface, I would say, 'I love you, my slimy little swamp monster.'"

"But, Mama, but, Mama, what if I were a **Green Alien** from Mars, and I ate bugs instead of peanut butter?"

"Then I would dress
you in colors that
showed off your
nice green skin . . .

and I would pack your lunch box with beetles and spiders and ants and grasshoppers and the tastiest bugs you ever had. And I would pack a note with all the bugs that said, 'I love you, little greenie. *Bon appétit.*'"

But, Mama, but, Mama, what if I were a **Cyclops**, and I had just one big, gigantic eye in the middle of my head?

"Then I would look right into your gigantic eye and say, 'I love you, my little cyclops,' and I would sing you a lullaby until your one gigantic eyelid got droopier and droopier, and it finally closed and you fell fast asleep."

I love you, Mama.

"And I love you, my wonderful child."